Snow dance

JF Ev   118980

Evans, Lezlie.
Wilton Public Library

DATE DUE

WDC			

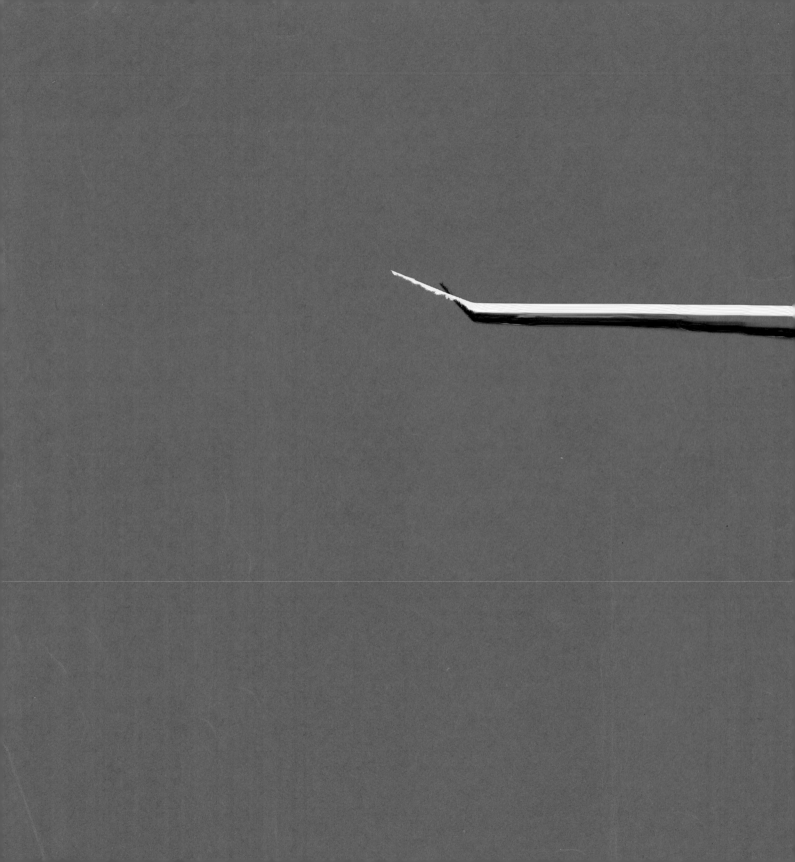

Snow Dance

Lezlie Evans

Illustrated by Cynthia Jabar

Houghton Mifflin Company
Boston 1997

For Andrew, Katie, Aubrey,
Megan, and Daniel . . . with love
— L.E.

— C.J.

Text copyright © 1997 by Lezlie Evans
Illustrations copyright © 1997 by Cynthia Jabar

For information about this and other Houghton Mifflin trade and
reference books and multimedia products, visit The Bookstore
at Houghton Mifflin on the World Wide Web at http://www.hmco.com/trade/.

The text of this book is set in 21 point Times Ten Roman.
The illustrations are watercolor, gouache and ink, reproduced in full color.

Library of Congress Cataloging-in-Publication Data
Evans, Lezlie.
Snow dance / by Lezlie Evans ; illustrated by Cynthia Jabar.
p. cm.
Summary: Children eagerly wait for the snow to begin to fall,
and when it does, they spend a day of fun playing in it.
ISBN 0-395-77849-2
[1. Winter — Fiction. 2. Snow — Fiction. 3. Stories in rhyme.]
I. Jabar, Cynthia, ill. II. Title.
PZ8.3.E915Sn 1997
[E] — dc20 95-43099 CIP AC

Manufactured in the United States of America
WOZ 10 9 8 7 6 5 4 3 2 1

Winter weary
cold and dreary
"How we wish that it would snow!"
Low clouds hover
sky is covered
"It just might, you never know."

Pressure's falling
forecast's calling
for a snowstorm late today.

"Find your warm boots
lay out snowsuits
do a snow dance and it may!"

Skipping, prancing
happy dancing
hoping snow will come our way.

We are whirling
swirling, twirling
begging flakes to come and stay.

Slowly drifting
downward sifting
falls a single flake of snow.

Snow grows thicker
coming quicker
now the flakes begin to flow.

Tongues outstretching
snowflakes catching
clinging to our hats and hair.

Spinning roundward
snow falls groundward
Spreading wonder everywhere.

Goose bumps showing
smoke-breath blowing
"Time to come in for the night.

Then while you sleep
snowflakes will keep
right on dancing till it's light."

Sun's rays streaming
white drifts gleaming
school is canceled for the day!

Bushes glimmer
sparkle, shimmer
"May we go outside and play?"

"Put warm clothes on
start with long johns
bundle up from head to toe.

Next come snowsuits
coats and big boots
hats and gloves, then off you go!"

Outside clomping
boot prints stomping
tasting, munching
fresh snow crunching

snow cakes baking
angel making
funny patterns in the snow.

Ice sheets cracking
snowman stacking
snowballs packing

friends attacking

frozen fingers
still we linger
having too much fun to go.

Red sled riding
downhill gliding
slipping, sliding

now colliding!

Rudolph noses
ice cold toeses
as we trudge home through the snow.

Inside filing

wet clothes piling
"Come and thaw out by the fire."

Mittens dripping
cocoa sipping
now we all begin to tire.

Day's now ending
night's descending
yet we're glad we've had the chance . . .

whirling, twirling
snowflakes swirling . . .
to be part of the snow dance.